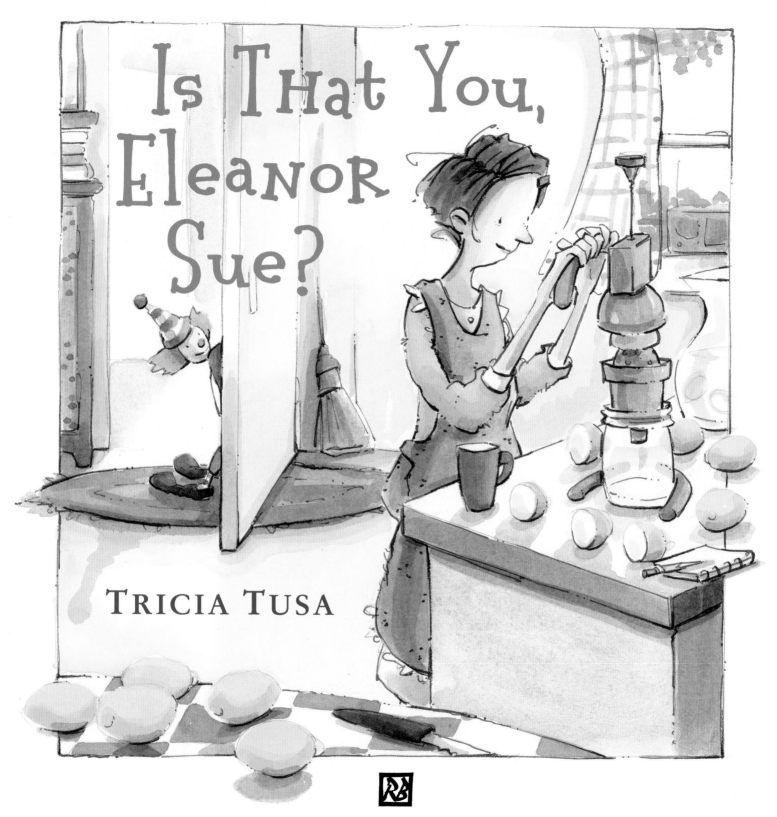

Is That You, Eleanor Sue?

Tricia Tusa

A NEAL PORTER BOOK
ROARING BROOK PRESS
NEW YORK

A Neal Porter Book
Published by Roaring Brook Press
Roaring Brook Press is a division of Holtzbrinck Publishing Holdings Limited Partnership
175 Fifth Avenue, New York, NY 10010
The art for this book was created using ink and watercolor, turnips, twigs, and raindrops.
mackids.com

Library of Congress Control Number: 2018932426
ISBN: 978-1-250-14323-5

Our books may be purchased in bulk for promotional, educational, or business use. Please
contact your local bookseller or the Macmillan Corporate and Premium Sales Department
at (800) 221-7945 ext. 5442 or by e-mail at MacmillanSpecialMarkets@macmillan.com.

First edition, 2018
Printed in China by RR Donnelley Asia Printing Solutions Ltd., Dongguan City, Guangdong Province

1 3 5 7 9 10 8 6 4 2

To Atticus, Scout, Jem, Calpurnia, Dill,
Tom Robinson, and Boo Radley

Today is Saturday, Eleanor Sue's favorite day to do her favorite thing— play dress-up.

So she climbs out her
bedroom window,

tiptoes over to the front door,

and rings the
doorbell.

Ding-dong.

Her mother answers the door.

"Well, hello. Can I help you?"

Eleanor Sue clears her throat. "Yes, yes, I am Mrs. McMuffins, your new neighbor. I thought I would come by to introduce myself and give you this gift."

Eleanor Sue hands her mother the garden gnome, plucked from the dandelion patch on the way to the front door.

"Oh my," says her mother. She invites the new neighbor in for tea.

Her mother asks how she likes the neighborhood.

Eleanor Sue responds with a sniff, "Well, it's okay. The sun shines right into my windows so I must wear sunglasses while I nap, and the birds sing so loudly down the chimney that I wear cotton in my ears, and I skinned my knee getting out of the bathtub, and my eyebrows hurt."

Her mother nodded as she listened. "I see," she said.

When Mrs. McMuffins left, she called out, "And by the way, my cat ran away. If you see her, let me know."

"I certainly will," her mother answered.
"Thank you for stopping by and for the gift!
I hope your eyebrows feel better soon."

Twenty minutes later, the doorbell rang.
"Hello," Eleanor Sue's mother said with surprise.
The witch said, "Hello. I was flying around up there and got caught in the wind and bumped right into your doorbell."

"My goodness. Please come in. May I fix you some lunch? I have never met a witch before."

"Well," the witch confided, "I used to be a little girl. I read a book of spells and learned how to make a recipe of old leaves, raindrops, turnips, and twigs. I drank it down and turned into a witch. Now I fly around the neighborhood on a broom and wait for Halloween to return."

"Fascinating," Eleanor Sue's mother said.

The witch left by way of the window.

Before she launched, she called out over her shoulder, "My uncle might come looking for me. He's a wizard and is 400 years old. Very wise."

And away the witch flew, down into the azalea bush below. "Goodbye. Please be careful . . . up there in those winds," her mother said.

Half an hour later, the doorbell rang again.
Eleanor Sue's mother looked out and saw
a man with a long, white beard.

"How do you do ma'm? I am a very old, wise wizard
and have come from far away. I have an important message
to share with you."

"Please come in, sir. Can I offer you a glass of water?"

He pondered this and said very mysteriously, "I have
swallowed oceans to get here. I might drown if I add one
more drop."

The wizard lifted his long, old finger into the air. "The secret to a happy and prosperous life," he said in a loud whisper, "is to touch your knees to your nose first thing every morning."

"Oh, like this?" her mother asked as she bent over.

"No, no, like this," the wizard said as he brought his ancient knee up to his very old nose.

"I must return now to where I have come from," he said.
Eleanor Sue's mother waved goodbye as he backed
himself into the deep bushes.

He called out, "Beware! A ferocious beast
may cross your path."
"Oh my," she said as she went back inside.

Well, sure enough, that doorbell rang and there stood a big, huge, humongous, gigantic, snarling, fang-dripping, sharp-clawed, bristly-furred, wet-nosed, crazy-eyed bear!!

Eleanor Sue's mother screamed and closed that door as quickly as she could.

She watched from the window as the bear
climbed up high into a tree, out of sight.

When that doorbell rang again, Eleanor Sue's
mother was greeted by a small delivery person.

"Sign right here, ma'am."
Daisies and begonias, flowers
that looked a lot like the ones growing
on the side of the house, were handed over.
"How lovely. For me?" she asked. "And
who could these be from?"
"Grandma," answered the delivery man.

"This morning I delivered doughnuts to the queen of a small island faraway across the sea. After that, a box of blue marbles to a centaur who lives deep in a forest under a large pile of leaves. I wore my shoes right through, ma'am. I've traveled that far."

Eleanor Sue's mother prepared a footbath of warm water, soap, and lotion.

"It's time for me to make my next delivery of chocolate-covered acorns to some squirrels near the equator. Goodbye."

It was not but ten minutes later that the doorbell rang again.

"Well, hello little kitty. Aren't you adorable. Why, you must be the new neighbor Mrs. McMuffin's missing cat."

"Meeooooooowwwww."
"My daughter Eleanor Sue loves kitty cats."

"Stay right there. I'll go get her." She headed down the hallway.

Meanwhile, Eleanor Sue ran as fast as she could

around the house and back through her bedroom window.

Her mother knocked on Eleanor Sue's bedroom door. "Hey there, punkin' pie. There's someone at the door you need to meet. The cutest cat."

"Not right now, Momma. I'm very busy."

"Oh, okay. He looks hungry. I'll fix him a bowl of milk. And grandma should be here soon."

Eleanor Sue climbed back out that window, running as fast as she could, alongside the house, and around the corner. Tripping over a rock, she fell flat on her face into a mud puddle.

She got up again, just in time . . .

. . . for that big bowl of warm milk.

"There you go. Drink up and hurry on home so that Mrs. McMuffins won't worry about you."

Eleanor Sue's mother closed the door.

Meanwhile, back in her room, Eleanor Sue pulled together the next outfit.

The doorbell rang.

It rang again,

and once more.

"Momma?!" Eleanor Sue cried out.
"Grandma?" asked Eleanor Sue's mother.

"Momma, you're not Grandma! Grandma is
Grandma. You are Momma!"

"Grandma, what are you doing here so early?"
Eleanor Sue's mother asked with a sly smile.

"No, Momma."
Before anything
else could be said,
the doorbell rang.

There stood Grandma carrying
a box of homemade cookies.

"How about that?" laughed
Grandma. "It looks as though
I am already here!"
Eleanor Sue wrapped her
arms around her.

While Grandma admired
her daughter's new look,

Eleanor Sue offered to
get the lemonade.

A few minutes later,
the doorbell rang.

"It's me,
Eleanor Sue."